The Sea Captain's
Compass

Written by Gary Urey

Illustrated by Carrie English

Sam & Sofia's Scooter Stories

First paperback edition printed in 2019 by Little Passports, Inc.
Copyright © 2019 Little Passports
All rights reserved
Book design by Carly Queen
Manufactured in China
10 9 8

Little Passports, Inc.
27 Maiden Lane, Suite 400, San Francisco, CA 94108
www.littlepassports.com
ISBN: 978-1-953148-02-5

Contents

1 The Compass 1
2 Philippe's Note 16
3 Room 64 24
4 Closed for Rénovation 36
5 The Portrait 46
6 Museum to Museum 54
7 The Age of Exploration 59
8 Monique's Note 67
9 The Cherub's Foot 81
10 Scooter Shutdown 93
11 Recharging 99

1
The Compass

Sofia yanked the lid off a plastic storage bin. A cloud of dust wafted into the air and drifted to her nose. She tried to stifle a sneeze, but it was too late.

"AAA . . . CHOO!"

"Bless you!" Sam said. "There's dust everywhere up here."

"I'm just pretending it's fairy dust," Sofia said, wiping her nose on her sleeve.

The attic was a cluttered mess. Stacks of musty cardboard boxes stood all around, holiday decorations littered the floor, and dozens of old paintings leaned against the slanted walls. The only light came from a small skylight above their heads.

Sam squinted through the shadows. "Did you find anything we can sell?" he asked.

Compass Court was hosting a neighborhood yard sale to benefit Compass Community Center. Sofia's mom had suggested they look in the attic for things to donate to the sale.

Suddenly, lights flashed in the darkness. Sam laughed and held up a small toy camera with bright flickering light bulbs.

"Another camera for your collection," Sofia

said with a giggle. Sam had a bunch of different cameras and was always taking pictures around the neighborhood.

Sam clicked off the lights on the toy and put it in his bag as Sofia reached inside the bin and grabbed an armful of her old dress-up clothes. There was a pair of fairy wings, a pointy green hat with a red feather, and a wooden sword.

"How about this?" Sam asked, holding up an old wooden box no bigger than a pack of crayons.

"What is it?"

Sam carefully opened the lid and his eyes lit up.

"Wow!" he said. "It's a compass."

"Well, we do live on Compass Court," Sofia said. She walked over to take a look. "I'm sure someone will want to buy it."

"It looks like an old seaman's compass," Sam said. "There's a picture of one in a book I'm reading."

A thin layer of brass encased the compass. It had a fancy starburst design, a needle, and points

marking four directions: north, south, east, and west.

"Wow," Sofia said. "It looks like it belongs in a museum."

Sam handed Sofia the old compass. She walked around the attic spinning in circles, kicking up little clouds of dust here and there. "It's broken," she said after a few spins. "Compasses are always supposed to point north. The needle on this one isn't moving. It's stuck between east and south."

"Can you fix it?" Sam asked.

Sofia loved tinkering with things. She had once turned paperclips into a metal hook to pull up a secret floorboard in Brazil, and she'd recently made a basket out of things she found in her pockets to save some eggs cooking in a Japanese hot spring.

"Maybe," Sofia said. "But I'll have to figure out a way to open it without breaking it."

Sam gently lifted the compass from the box. "Check out the design on the back. It looks like it's engraved."

Sofia looked closely and saw a shield surrounding a ship's anchor and two soaring seagulls. A sparkle of excitement tingled her heart.

"I've seen this design somewhere before," Sofia said. "Follow me."

The two climbed down the steep stairs from the attic and headed to Papai's art studio. Sofia's dad was an artist, and his studio was one of Sofia's favorite spots in the house. A large bay window flooded the room with sunshine, and the smell of oil paints filled the air. Clumps of dried modeling clay speckled the floor. A table stacked with blank canvases and paintbrushes sat in the corner.

Sofia searched the art hanging on the walls until she found a sketch of a man in a small frame. He was holding a book... and a compass!

"That's Captain Philippe," Sofia said, "my great-great-great-great-grandfather."

"The compass in the sketch looks like ours," Sam said. He pulled one of his cameras from his messenger bag and snapped a picture of the sketch. **Click-click!**

"Look at the mark on the book he's holding," Sofia said. "It's the same as the symbol on the back of the compass!"

Sofia explained the family legend to Sam: Philippe had been a ship captain and explorer who sailed all over the world. His adventures took him to China, India, and South America, where he finally settled in Brazil.

"Wow," Sam said, looking at the compass. "You're related to a real explorer, like Ferdinand Magellan. He crossed the Pacific Ocean before anyone else in Europe. Or like Jeanne Baret! She was the first woman to circumnavigate the world."

"I always thought the stories about Philippe were tall tales," Sofia said. "But if this is really his compass, the stories might be true after all! And some of them were full of danger."

"What kind of danger?" Sam asked.

"Battles with pirates, shipwrecks, hurricanes, shark attacks, and—"

SLAM!

The pair jumped. They turned to see Sofia's dad plopping down a bag of art supplies on a nearby table.

"Sorry," Papai said. "I didn't mean to startle you kids."

"Look what we found," Sofia said, handing Papai the compass.

Papai carefully examined the unmoving needle and tarnished brass. He turned it over and looked at the design engraved on the back.

"I haven't seen this in years," he said. "Where did you find it?"

"Up in the attic inside a box," Sofia answered. "The one Avó mailed to us from Brazil."

"My friends and I played with this compass when I was a kid back in São Paulo," Papai said. "We wanted to be explorers and swashbucklers like Philippe."

Sam pointed to Philippe's sketch. "It looks like the same compass in the drawing."

"That's because it is the same," Papai said with a smile. "And the shield on the back with the anchor and seagulls? That's our family crest."

Sofia looked at the drawing of Philippe. He sat in a chair, wearing a fancy jacket and a vest. Scrawled across the bottom of the sketch in charcoal were the words *étude pour le portrait du Capitaine de Fluerieu.*

étude pour le portrait du Capitaine de Fluerieu

"What do those words mean?" Sofia asked.

"That's French," Papai said. "It means this is a study for Captain Philippe's portrait. The sketch was probably used as a practice drawing for a painted portrait."

"Where's the finished portrait?" Sam asked.

"I wish I knew," Papai said, shaking his head. "The sketch is from the late eighteenth century. The portrait might not even exist anymore.

Maybe—" Papai grabbed a paintbrush and swished it through the air like a sword "—it was stolen by pirates!"

Sam's eyes lit up. "Pirates!?"

Sofia giggled.

"One morning many, many years ago," Papai said, bringing his voice down low, "Captain Philippe and his men woke to find themselves under attack by pirates! The pirate ship was much bigger and had more weapons and a larger crew than Captain Philippe's, but he refused to surrender."

Papai hopped up onto the table with his paintbrush sword and pulled Sam and Sofia up with him.

"Cannon fire blasted the hull!" he cried. "Sword fights raged. Philippe and his men fought bravely but soon realized their ship was lost. To avoid capture, Philippe and his men leapt into the ocean." Papai jumped from the table. Sam and Sofia followed, laughing. The three of them lay flat on the floor, pretending to drift on the ocean. "They floated for days on a rickety raft without food or water, fighting off bloodthirsty sharks, until washing ashore. And where'd they wash up, Sofia?"

"In Brazil!" Sofia said.

"That's right," said Papai, helping the two back to their feet. "That's how my family ended up in São Paulo."

"That's such an exciting story!" Sam said. "And it happened to one of your relatives."

"It is a pretty good one, isn't it?" Papai said.

"But is it true?" Sofia asked.

Papai put his paintbrush back in its place. "It's

hard to know. Philippe lived so long ago. The logbook he's holding in the sketch could give us some answers. But like his portrait, no one knows if it still exists after all these years."

Papai rummaged through a cabinet. He opened a folder, plucked out a sheet of paper, and handed it to Sofia. The paper had dozens of names all connected to each other in a diagram.

"This is our family tree," Papai said.

Sofia studied the paper, tracing her name through the centuries all the way back to Philippe.

Papai handed Sofia the compass. "Your *avó*

gave me the compass when I was your age. I think it's time for me to pass it on to you."

"Thanks, Papai," Sofia said, giving her father a hug. She looked down at the compass and its unmoving needle.

"It's always been broken," Papai said. "I'd love to see it working again, but it's special even as it is." He grabbed a blank canvas from the table, placed it on an easel, and started sorting through his brushes.

Sofia glanced at the sketch, slipped the compass into her pocket, and whispered into Sam's ear.

"We need to go to the lab," she said. *"Vamos!"*

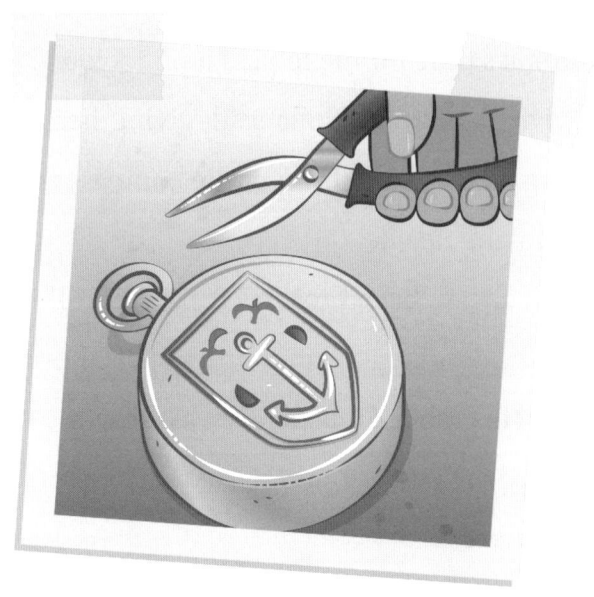

2
Philippe's Note

Sofia and Sam raced across Compass Court to Sam's house and slipped into his garage.

"This is one of my favorite places in the whole world," Sofia said with a sparkle in her heart.

Sam's Aunt Charlie was a scientist and

inventor, and she'd converted the garage into a workshop. It was full of beakers, test tubes, flasks, glass rods, and countless gadgets. There was a large telescope for studying the stars, and a machine used to determine the age of rocks over a million years old. She even had shards of rock collected from a meteorite.

"Okay," Sam said. "What do we need from the lab?"

"You asked me if I could fix the compass," Sofia said. "Well, I want to fix it for Papai. We might not be able to find Philippe's portrait, but maybe I can get his compass working again."

"I bet you can," Sam said.

They stepped over to a long worktable. Sofia slipped on a pair of safety glasses and pulled the compass from her pocket. She turned it over in her hands.

"How will you get it open without breaking it?" Sam asked.

Sofia narrowed her eyes like she always did when trying to figure out a problem. She looked at the back of the compass. "These two notches," she said, "may have something to do with opening the compass. But how?"

Sofia set the compass on the worktable.

"Turning... or maybe twisting... rotating," Sofia mumbled to herself.

Careful not to scratch the metal, Sofia grabbed a pair of needle-nose pliers and placed one of the tool's tips into each of the notches. She turned the pliers counterclockwise, and after a little shimmying, the back of the compass twisted open.

Sofia lifted the metal piece, uncovering a folded piece of paper lodged inside. She used a pair of tweezers to gently pull out the paper. The compass's needle began to wobble.

"You fixed it!" Sam said.

"The compass wasn't broken after all," Sofia said, pulling off her goggles. "This paper was jamming the needle."

"Captain Philippe would be proud," Sam said with a smile.

The yellowed paper was thin and brittle. Sofia carefully unfolded it, revealing faded words written in splotchy ink.

"It looks like some kind of note or letter," Sofia said.

"What's the language?" Sam asked. "Is it French, like the words on the sketch?"

"It's definitely not Portuguese or Japanese," Sofia said. "Let's ask the scooter."

The scooter was Aunt Charlie's most impressive invention. It had a candy-apple-red finish, chrome handlebars, and big black tires. A large touch screen fit snugly between the handlebars. The scooter was their ticket to adventure, and the touch screen was full of information, like a supercomputer.

Sofia put the compass back together and climbed onto the scooter's seat. She tapped the touch screen, found the **SCAN MODE** setting, and pressed the note against the screen. A few seconds later, the computer had translated the note into English.

> My dear François.
> The Louvre is expecting my portrait for the grand event.
> As I am now old, please make sure my sailing logbook is kept safe for future generations.
> Return to Brazil soon!
> Your loving father, Philippe

Sofia plucked the family tree from her pocket. "Look!" she said. "Philippe had a son named François! This was definitely written by my great-great-great-great-grandfather!"

"You know what this means?" Sam asked.

"Philippe's portrait might be hanging in the Louvre," Sofia answered. "The museum might also have his logbook!"

Sam hopped onto the back of the scooter behind Sofia. "Are you thinking what I'm thinking?"

"I'm thinking it's time for some adventuring," Sofia answered.

A globe appeared on the touch screen with a flashing message.

Sofia looked over her shoulder at Sam. He nodded and she tapped out a reply to the question on the screen:

Louvre Museum, Paris

The scooter's powerful engine rumbled to life beneath them. Its headlights and taillights lit up. The touch screen shined like a movie projector in a dark theater. Glowing light encircled them, flashing and glittering. Static electricity made the hair on their heads stand on end.

Sam held on and counted down, "Five . . . four . . . three . . . two . . ."

Sofia pushed the glowing green button with her finger. "*Vamos!*"

Whiz . . . Zoom . . . FOOP!

3
Room 64

Sofia took several long, slow breaths. Her head was spinning and her stomach felt slightly queasy. The lights from the scooter were still shimmering, but Sofia and Sam weren't in Aunt Charlie's garage anymore. They were on a busy city street.

"We're... in Paris!" Sofia heard Sam say behind her.

Sofia blinked the stars from her eyes and looked around. She'd never get used to the way the scooter zoomed them across the world. It sort of felt like flying, except it happened all at once. There was no place they couldn't explore with the help of Aunt Charlie's amazing invention.

"Wow," Sofia said in awe. "Paris is huge."

Large city blocks stretched before them, full of wide streets, green parks, and a gently flowing river. Crowds of people filled the sidewalks.

Sofia steered the scooter to a curb. They parked next to a row of bicycles, scooters, and motorcycles. People were strolling around a beautiful building made of carved stone.

"It's the Louvre!" Sam said, taking out his camera. He held the lens to his eyes and took a picture. **Click-click!**

"I've always wanted to come here."

"Uh-oh," Sofia said.

"What is it?" asked Sam.

Sofia had just noticed something on the scooter's screen. "The scooter's battery," she said. "It's already low!"

"It must not have been plugged in back at Aunt Charlie's lab," Sam said. "I think the screen uses power even when no one is riding the scooter. Something to do with the mapping system."

"Then we don't have much time," Sofia said. "Quick! Let's go find Philippe's portrait and logbook."

Sam followed Sofia through a courtyard twice the size of a soccer field and into a large glass pyramid, which was the entrance of the museum. A spiral staircase shuttled them into the museum's lobby.

"This place is massive," Sam said. "How are we ever going to find the portrait? We don't even know for sure if it's here."

Disappointment panged Sofia's heart. Sam was right. The museum was overwhelming, and with the scooter's battery so low, they didn't have much time to look.

"We need to ask someone," Sofia said. "Over here."

The information desk was busy, with several people waiting in line. Sofia looked at a big clock ticking time away next to a poster with an image of a ship. It was so hard standing in line when they had such little time to explore. When it was finally Sofia and Sam's turn,

they rushed to the counter.

A woman looked down at them. "Welcome to the Louvre. My name is Josiane. How may I assist you?"

"We're trying to find out if you have a certain painting at the museum."

"Name of *artiste, s'il vous plaît?*"

"Um . . . I'm not sure," Sofia answered. "But I know the name of the man in the portrait. Can you find it that way?"

"This is Sofia," Sam added, nodding to his

friend. "She's his great-great-great-great-granddaughter. We're also looking for his ship's logbook."

"Let me try to look him up," Josiane said. How do you spell his last name?"

Sofia said each letter slowly.

"F - L - U - E - R - I - E - U."

Josiane typed into her computer and hit Enter. "I'm sorry. Nothing's coming up."

"Nothing?" Sofia asked.

Josiane shook her head. "Are you sure that's how it's spelled?"

Sam lifted his camera and pulled up his picture of Philippe's sketch. The letters along the bottom spelled the name Fluerieu. "That's how it's spelled," Sam said.

"I'm sorry," Josiane said. "It's not here. Can I help you with something else?"

Sofia hung her head. She pulled the compass from her pocket and looked at the anchor on the back. Her eyes narrowed, and then she glanced up at the poster next to the clock. Beneath the picture of the ship were the words **Seafarers and Explorers Exhibition Reopening Soon!** Sofia felt a little twinge of hope. If Philippe's portrait and logbook were at the Louvre, they had to be in that exhibit.

Sofia leaned over the counter closer to Josiane. "Can you tell us where the Seafarers and Explorers collection is, please?"

Josiane shook her head and said, "It's not ready. They are closing the exhibit today for extensive *rénovations*. If you don't have any other questions, I'm sorry, but I have other guests to help."

"Please tell us where it is," Sofia said. "We have to check. We've come a long way and we're not leaving without finding that painting!"

Josiane squinted at her. "You are a bold little girl," she said with a pout. "I like that." Her lips curved into a smile. She leaned down further and whispered, "The Sully Wing, first floor, Room 64. But you better hurry! Renovations begin this afternoon and guests aren't allowed in the area."

"*Merci!*" Sofia said.

"Which way is the Sully Wing?" Sam asked.

Sofia held up the compass. "Philippe would have used this," she said, wiggling her eyebrows.

"Very funny," Sam said.

Josiane pointed to a large escalator. "The exhibit is that way on the first floor. Now go! Quick!"

The kids bounded up to the first floor. Swarms of people crowded the exquisite hall. Some posed for pictures while others stared in awe at the beautiful statues, sculptures, and paintings. Sofia knew that Sam wanted to look at them all, but she was on a mission to find Room 64.

The two weaved through the museumgoers.

They finally found the Sully Wing and hurried past exhibits of ancient bronze statues, Greek ceramics, and Egyptian art.

"There it is!" Sam said.

Sofia looked down the hall and saw the number **64** above a closed door. Her heart pounded with anticipation as she approached the door. They'd believed, traveled across the world, and now the portrait was possibly just feet away. Sofia reached out and jerked the handle downward, but it wouldn't budge.

"It's locked!" she said.

4
Closed for Renovation

Sam pointed to a sign hanging on the wall. It had the same image of a ship as the poster in the lobby. It also had a message:

Exhibit Room 64 temporarily closed for renovation. Check website for updates.

"We're so close," Sofia said, clenching her fists.

"Maybe . . . but maybe not," Sam said. "We don't even know if his portrait and logbook are really here."

"Now we'll never know for sure. At least not until they renovate the room."

"I'm sorry, Sofia," Sam said. "Would it make you feel better to explore other parts of the museum? Maybe it would distract you." He looked down the hall toward the exhibits and back to Sofia. "And who knows, maybe the portrait is actually somewhere else. We can keep looking for it along the way."

"Yeah, I guess," Sofia said. She reached out and jiggled the doorknob to Room 64 one last time, then she gave the door a hard knock. Just as Sam was stepping away, a deep voice echoed from behind the door.

"Sorry," the voice said, making Sam and Sofia jump. "Exhibit is *fermé*. Closed."

"I—um . . ." Sofia cleared her throat. "I just need five minutes."

The door flung open. A museum worker looked down at her and Sam. He was tall and wore a nametag that read *Jean-Luc*.

"Oh," he said, disappointed. "I thought you were my staff. I'm missing some materials."

He turned to close the door, but Sofia reached out and grabbed it. He looked down at her again, even more annoyed.

"I know you're closed, but I'm looking for the portrait of my great-great-great-great-grandfather," Sofia said. "And the logbook from his ship. Josiane at the information desk said they might be here."

Jean-Luc's forehead furrowed as he decided

whether or not to let them in.

"We'll only be a minute," Sam said.

Jean-Luc peered down the hall, looked at his watch, and shook his head.

"*Non*," he said. "I'm sorry. I cannot let you inside. Enjoy the rest of the museum."

The door slammed shut. Sofia heard a click as Jean-Luc turned the lock on the other side.

"*Argh!*" Sofia said. "We need to get inside this room!"

The Louvre was an enormous museum. It was full of all kinds of exhibits, and the one room that might hold the answer to Sofia's family history was right in front of her, but off-limits.

"I need to think," Sofia said.

The two friends walked down the hallway from Room 64 to the Egyptian Antiquities section. Sofia pulled the compass from her pocket as they stopped in front of an exhibit called the Seated Scribe. It was a statue of a man sitting cross-legged and holding a scroll. Sam took a picture—**click-click!**—but Sofia couldn't think of anything but Philippe. She wondered if the man with the scroll was someone's great-great-great-great-grandfather.

"I don't think I'm going to enjoy any of the art," Sofia said. "I have to know if Philippe's portrait and logbook are on the other side of that door."

Sam looked at his camera and then at his friend. "Okay," he said. "Then it's time to come up with a plan."

"No, you should go explore the museum," Sofia said. "You love art. You should enjoy it."

"You're my best friend," Sam said. "Where you go, I go." He stuffed his camera into his messenger bag and put on his thinking face. "Now how are we going to get through that door?"

Sofia beamed at Sam. There was no one else she'd rather have by her side on this adventure. Well, except maybe a locksmith.

Sofia was about to ask Sam for her notebook so she could list ideas for what to do next, but something caught her eye. Down the hall, she saw a man pushing a big cart. It was filled with tools, thick tarps, and large boxes. The man was dressed in crocodile-green coveralls, and Sofia could hear a ticking sound growing louder as he came close. She squinted and saw a pocket watch hanging from his belt.

When Sofia looked at the sign on the side of the cart, she gasped.

Sofia ducked behind the Egyptian statue, pulling Sam with her.

"Hey!" Sam said, straightening his shirt.

"That man is going into Room 64!" Sofia whispered.

Sam leaned around the statue and used the zoom lens on his camera to get a better view.

"We have to get inside that cart," Sofia said. "We need a distraction, and quick!"

Sam rummaged through his messenger bag.

He looked up and smiled. From his bag, he pulled the toy camera they'd found in Sofia's attic. Sam clicked the button on the side of the camera and its lights flashed to life.

"We can use this," Sam said, and Sofia smiled.

He handed the camera to Sofia, and when the man in green was looking the other way, Sam whispered, "Now!"

Sofia popped out from behind the statue and threw the camera. It clattered down the hall,

bouncing on the ground as its lights flickered off the walls. The crocodile man turned toward the noise and took a few steps toward the flashing lights. Sofia and Sam saw their chance. They dashed into the hallway and dove into the cart. Sofia unfurled one of the tarps and threw it over both of them.

Everything went dark. Sofia could hear her heart pounding in her ears. Dust from the blankets made her nose twitch, but she couldn't move a muscle or they might get caught. Sofia tried not to breathe. She heard the ticking of the man's pocket watch get louder as his footsteps came back to the cart. She expected the man to start pushing them, but nothing happened.

Why weren't they moving? Did the man suspect something?

Sofia peered nervously at Sam under the tarp. They waited, frozen, listening to the pocket watch **tick-tock-tick-tock-tick-**

tock-tick-tock . . .

5
The Portrait

Just when Sofia was sure the crocodile man had found them, the rickety cart lurched forward.

The sound of the cart's wheels mixed with the ticking of the pocket watch as the man in green pushed them down the hallway. Sam's breathing was heavy but low. A bead of sweat rolled down Sofia's temple. She felt for the compass in her front pocket and wondered what direction they were going. North, south, east, or west?

"The compass is leading us to Philippe," she whispered. "I can feel it in my bones."

The cart made an abrupt stop. There was a loud rustling sound as a large hand reached into the cart, making all the muscles in Sofia's body clench. She grabbed Sam's elbow and rolled to the side as the hand moved around, grabbed a set of keys, and lifted back out of the cart.

Sofia let out a relieved breath. She could hear the keys jingling and the sound of a door opening. They were on the move again, but for a shorter time.

"Wrap the paintings in this *couverture*," a voice said nearby.

"That's Jean-Luc," Sofia whispered to Sam.

"Let's haul the paintings we've already wrapped down to storage," Jean-Luc continued. "Then we'll come for the rest."

Sofia and Sam stayed as still as the Egyptian statue they'd seen earlier. Sofia was convinced they would be discovered at any moment. They waited while people moved around them, and eventually, when the footsteps and the ticking of the man's pocket watch grew silent, they slowly peeked out from under the tarp.

"I can't believe that worked," Sam said, smoothing his hair.

"We have to be quick," Sofia said as the two climbed out of the cart. "You heard the man. They'll be back soon to take away the rest of the paintings."

Sofia and Sam looked around Room 64. They saw sculptures and statues of beautiful mermaids, anchors, and ships. Dozens of elegant portraits

hung on the walls inside fancy frames. Crates, blankets, rolls of bubble wrap, and cardboard boxes were scattered across the floor. With the exhibit lights dimmed, it reminded Sofia of her attic back home.

"Come on," Sofia said. "I know Philippe's portrait is here somewhere."

Sofia searched one side of the room and Sam the other. Sofia carefully studied each portrait, trying to find her distant relative. Mixed with the portraits of sea captains and explorers were paintings of ships, tropical islands, crashing waves, and skiffs tied to wooden docks. Sofia scanned the paintings. None of them resembled the sketch of Philippe.

"I don't see him," Sam said from across the room.

"Keep looking," Sofia said. "Time's running out!"

The two worked their way around Room 64 until they met back where they had started.

There was only one section of wall left, on the far side of the room. Sofia and Sam walked over together, and there was Sofia's *papai* looking back at them.

Except it wasn't Papai. It was Captain Philippe!

"Wow," Sofia said.

"That has to be him!" said Sam. "He looks just like your dad!"

Hanging on the wall was a large painting of a distinguished-looking man. The colors were vibrant and lifelike. Philippe held a compass and logbook like in the sketch in Papai's art studio. Unlike the other paintings hanging inside fancy gold frames, a modest

wooden border surrounded Philippe's portrait. But that didn't matter to Sofia one bit. It was the most beautiful piece of art she had ever seen.

"The family resemblance is strong," Sam said. He raised his camera and took pictures of the portrait. **Click-click!**

"I can't believe we found it," Sofia said, almost jumping with excitement.

"Check this out," Sam said, pointing to a transparent board beneath the painting.

Captain Philippe de Fleurieu
French Trader and Explorer

He commanded a three-mast ship called La Mouette—The Seagull.

"Wait a minute," Sofia said. "Can I see the photo of Papai's sketch?"

Sam thumbed back through some photos

and handed his camera to Sofia. She looked at the sketch on the camera's screen and back to the plaque on the wall.

"The name is spelled *F-L-U-E-R-I-E-U* on the sketch but spelled *F-L-E-U-R-I-E-U* here," she said. "The first *E* and *U* are switched around. That must be why Josiane couldn't find it in the database!"

"Two little letters gave us all that trouble," Sam said, shaking his head.

"Oh, wait," Sofia said. "His logbook! I almost forgot. Do you think it's here somewhere? That's what will tell us about his travels."

"You!" A loud voice bellowed from behind them, and Sofia nearly leapt out of her shoes.

6
Museum to Museum

Sofia looked up to see Jean-Luc glaring at her.

"I told you this room was closed for *rénovations!*" he barked.

"The man in this painting is my great-great-

great-great-grandfather," Sofia said.

"Impossible," Jean-Luc said. He stomped over to them and looked at the plaque under the painting. "This is a portrait of Captain Philippe de Fleurieu, a French trader and explorer from the eighteenth century." He looked down his nose at Sofia. "This man is your great-great-great-grandfather?"

"Four 'greats,' actually, but yes," Sofia said. She pulled the compass from her pocket and handed it to Jean-Luc. "Look. It's the same compass that's in the painting. It's been in my family for generations. See the crest?"

The harshness slowly melted from Jean-Luc's face as he compared the compass in his hand to the one in the painting.

"They certainly look the same," Jean-Luc said after a moment.

"That's because they are," Sam said, pulling out his camera. "Look at this picture I took. It's

the practice sketch for Philippe's portrait."

"My Papai has it hanging in his studio," Sofia added. "He's an artist himself."

Jean-Luc took the camera. He compared the sketch and painting carefully.

"Remarkable," Jean-Luc said. "You are absolutely correct. The sketch and the portrait of Monsieur de Fleurieu match perfectly. We must have this for our Prints and Drawings collection."

Sam nudged Sofia. "The logbook," he said in a whisper.

"Right!" Sofia turned to Jean-Luc. "Let's make a deal."

Jean-Luc furrowed his eyebrows. "What kind of deal?"

"I'll get you a copy of the sketch if you can tell us where to find the logbook in the painting. Is it on display somewhere in the museum?"

"*Non*," Jean-Luc said, shaking his head. "Something like that would be at the *Musée National de la Marine*."

"What's that? Sam asked.

"The National Maritime Museum. It's not too far from here, along the Seine River."

"We saw the river when the scooter arrived!" Sam said.

"Now, when will I receive a copy of the sketch?" Jean-Luc asked.

"I'll send it to you," Sofia said. "Promise!"

They thanked Jean-Luc and rushed out of Room 64.

"No running in the museum!" he called after them.

7

The Age of Exploration

Sofia and Sam ran to the scooter, hopped on board, and tapped the touchscreen.

"Pull up the Maritime Museum," Sam said.

A few seconds later, a street map came up with turn-by-turn directions. The National Maritime

Museum was west of the Louvre along the Seine River. Sofia revved the scooter's engine, and they cruised a block up the street and crossed a bridge over the Seine. As they rode, Sofia thought of Philippe navigating all around the world with only a compass. The very same one she now had stuffed in her pocket.

"The touch screen says the source of the Seine is near a city called Dijon in northeastern France," Sam said.

"Dijon sounds like the mustard Papai spreads on his sandwiches," Sofia said.

"The screen says something else," Sam said. "The scooter's battery is down to thirty-two percent."

"Then we need to hurry and find the logbook."

With a roar of the engine, they crossed another bridge over the Seine, called the Pont d'Iena. A beautiful park with tall trees, green lawns, and water fountains lay before them. A large sign pointed toward the *Musée National de la Marine*.

"There's the entrance," Sofia said.

They parked the scooter and bounded up the museum's stone steps, walked up to a set of revolving doors, and stopped. The doors were locked.

"Why," Sofia said, jiggling a door handle, "is everything closed? It's another dead end!"

Through the doors, she could see a sunny gallery inside displaying maritime paintings, old wooden ship figureheads, giant glass lenses from lighthouses, and a gold dolphin figure.

"Look," Sam said, pointing to a sign on a nearby stand. "We can't get inside the museum, but it looks like there's some kind of event out back."

"I bet Philippe sailed on a ship just like the one in the exhibit," Sofia said. "Okay, let's check it out. Maybe we'll get some clues."

La Baleine stood in a large open space added to the back of the museum. The ship was enormous! There were six cannons, three on each side of the ship, and big billowing sails stretched above them, attached to tall masts. As they waited to board, Sofia could see old barrels, wooden chests, and thick ropes scattered around the deck.

When it was their turn to board the ship, Sofia and Sam walked up a set of steps to the upper deck. A museum tour guide dressed in breeches, a baggy white shirt, and a blue bandanna led a tour group below deck. Sofia was about to join them when she saw a large wooden wheel toward the back of the ship.

"Look at this," Sofia said, running to the ship's wheel.

She gripped the wheel and thought of Philippe. He would have stood in front of a wheel just like this for months on end, steering the *Seagull* as it crossed the endless blue ocean.

"Take a picture of me at the helm," Sofia said.

"Aye aye, captain," Sam said with a giggle. Sofia grabbed the compass from her pocket and held it high in the air with a smile. **Click-click!**

"Will you take a picture of me, too?" Sam asked.

"Behind the wheel?" Sofia asked.

"No," Sam said, pointing into the sky. "Up in the crow's nest."

Sam handed Sofia the camera and he slowly climbed the rigging. Sofia walked to get a better view, set the compass on a rail, and started snapping pictures. He didn't get ten feet before a deep voice called out to him.

"Come down from there! *Ce n'est pas permis.*"

Sofia turned to see the tour guide.

"No climbing allowed," the guide said with a stern look on his face.

"Sorry," Sam called back. "Climbing down!"

Sofia rushed over to help Sam down. When his feet hit the deck, the tour guide turned back to his group and Sofia let out a breath. The last thing in the world she wanted was for them to get in trouble before they had a chance to look for the logbook.

"Come on," Sofia whispered to Sam. "Let's find an information desk and ask for help."

Sofia handed the camera back to Sam as they turned toward the ship's steps. She reached into her pocket... and didn't feel Philippe's compass! Panic sliced through her body.

"Oh no," Sofia said. "The compass! It's gone!"

8
Monique's Note

Tears rimmed Sofia's eyes. She thought of Papai. He had trusted her to take care of the compass. Besides the portrait, it was the family's only link to Philippe, and now the heirloom was gone.

"It has to be in one of your pockets," Sam said.

"I've checked them a dozen times!" Sofia cried. "I can't find it anywhere!"

She took several slow breaths.

"When was the last time you saw it?" Sam asked.

Sofia paced the floor, her pulse racing.

"Um . . ." she said. "I . . . I think I set it down somewhere when you asked me to take your picture."

"*Excusez-moi?*" a voice called out from behind. "Did you forget something?"

Sofia turned and saw a girl about their age wearing a dark shirt and a nametag. She was holding brochures in one hand and a small wooden box in the other.

"The compass! You found it!" Sofia said.

The girl handed Sofia the compass. "You put it down on the railing," she said.

"Thank you!" Sofia said, giving the girl a hug.

"This is my great-great-great-great-grandfather Philippe's compass. It's over two hundred years old."

"Maybe even a little older than that," the girl said. "The symbol of the anchor and two seagulls is a very unique design."

"This is Sam," Sofia said, nodding to her friend. "I'm Sofia."

"My name's Émilie. My *père* is the head curator of the museum. I'm going to be a curator too someday."

"We're looking for Philippe's old sailing logbook from the seventeen-hundreds," Sofia said. "Captain Philippe de Fleurieu. The logbook should have the same anchor and seagulls design as the compass. We were hoping it might be on display here at the museum."

"We don't have any old seafaring logbooks currently on display," Émilie said. "But we have dozens of similar items down in storage."

"But the museum's closed," Sofia said.

"It is," said Émilie. "But I have the key. Come with me."

Sofia's heart tingled with hope as she and Sam followed Émilie off the ship and to a door marked *Réservé aux employés*. Émilie unlocked the door with a quick flick of her wrist, and the three walked into the museum.

Sofia and Sam followed Émilie down two flights of stairs to a large, well-lit basement. There were several rows of shelves stacked with different artifacts. Sofia noticed old paintings, swords, rusty bells, antique telescopes, and several wooden ships' wheels.

Émilie stopped in front of a row of dusty filing cabinets. "How do you spell the name of your relative?"

Sofia shot Sam a glance, remembering all the confusion caused by the different spellings of Philippe's last name.

"It's either Philippe de Fleurieu or de Fluerieu," Sofia said. "We've seen the *U* and *E* switched around."

Sofia crossed her fingers as Émilie rifled through a filing cabinet. At any moment Émilie could yank out Philippe's logbook and Sofia would finally have proof of his adventures.

"I'm sorry," Émilie said. "I'm not finding anything under the spellings you gave me for Philippe de Fleurieu."

Sofia felt deflated. She thought Philippe's logbook would be here, but they'd reached another dead end.

"However," Émilie added, "I did find something under the name Monique de Fleurieu."

"That name sounds familiar," Sofia said, excitement flooding back to her. She pulled her family tree from Sam's messenger bag, where she'd stored it. "Look!" she said. "Philippe's son was named François, and François had a daughter named Monique!"

"We're on the right track," Sam said.

"Monique was Philippe's granddaughter!"

Émilie pulled a slip of paper from the filing cabinet, read it carefully, then stepped to a nearby shelf. She pulled a cardboard box from a small stack, placed it on a table, and slipped on a pair of white gloves. Then she turned to Sam and Sofia and handed them each a pair of gloves as well.

"We must be very careful when touching an *objet d'art*," Emilie said.

Sofia put on her gloves as Émilie carefully removed

the contents from the box. There were ancient sundials, medals, handmade tools, and a thick stack of loose, old-looking papers. One by one, Émilie went through the pages in the box. Sofia's heart thumped with anticipation.

"Here it is," Émilie said, plucking a page from the stack. She carefully unfolded the paper for Sam and Sofia to see.

"It has my family crest!" Sofia said.

"Can I take a picture of it?" Sam asked, and Émilie nodded.

Sam raised his camera. **Click-click!**

"But it's not a logbook," Sam said, lowering his lens. "It's only a letter."

Sofia very carefully took the page from Émilie and scrunched up her eyebrows. Sam was right. The family crest was the same, but it wasn't a book. It was just a short note written in French.

"Can you tell us what it says?" Sofia asked. She placed the page on the table and pulled her notebook from Sam's messenger bag.

Émilie translated the note and, as she did, Sofia rewrote it.

"The cherubs?" Sam asked. "That doesn't sound clear to me."

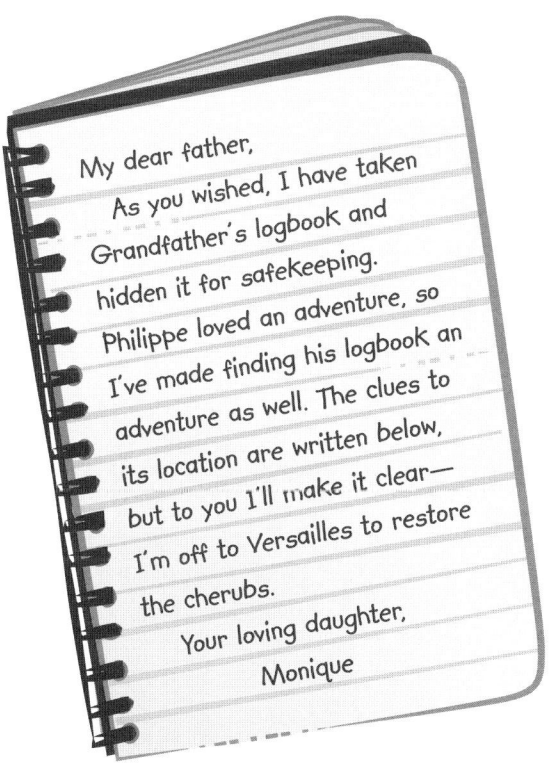

My dear father,
As you wished, I have taken Grandfather's logbook and hidden it for safekeeping.
Philippe loved an adventure, so I've made finding his logbook an adventure as well. The clues to its location are written below, but to you I'll make it clear—I'm off to Versailles to restore the cherubs.
Your loving daughter,
Monique

"What are the clues?" Sofia asked Émilie, and

Émilie kept translating.

"That's a really nice poem," Sam said, "but I have no idea what it means."

From the Cour d'Honneur . . .

Walk west to the oranges,
north-west to the mirror.
Stroll north and the giant
sun god will appear here.
The Spring Fountain follows,
to the opposite of west.
Look close for the cherub
marked with our dear crest.

"From the note, it sounds like Monique was a restoration artist," Émilie said. "She was probably helping to restore a cherub sculpture at the Palace of Versailles."

"Maybe she hid the logbook near the cherubs?" Sofia asked.

"The clues might make more sense once we're there," Sam said.

"What does *core . . . d . . . honn . . . er* mean?" Sofia asked.

"*Cour d'Honneur* means Courtyard of Honor," Émilie explained. "It is the main entrance for the Palace of Versailles." She opened a nearby drawer full of pamphlets and brochures and handed Sam a map of the palace. "The grounds are quite extensive. Hopefully, this map will help you find what you are looking for."

"How far is the palace from here?" Sofia asked.

"About twenty kilometers," Émilie answered.

"Thank you for your help, Émilie," Sofia said.

"Of course," said Émilie. "Now you'd better hurry. The palace grounds are quite large."

Sam raised his camera again. "One last thing," he said. "Say cheese!"

Sofia and Émilie posed for the camera. "*Fromage!*" Sofia said, smiling, and Émilie laughed. **Click-click!**

After saying their goodbyes, Sam and Sofia ran out of the museum and back to the scooter. Sofia hopped on the seat and Sam slid in behind her. She quickly tapped the touch screen and typed out **Palace of Versailles.**

"Oh no," Sofia said.

"What is it?" Sam asked.

"The scooter's battery. It's only at fifteen percent now."

"If the battery completely dies, we're stuck

here," said Sam. "Maybe we should go home."

Sofia bit her bottom lip. She'd been right about the portrait being in Room 64, and now after talking to Émilie she felt in her bones that Philippe's logbook was somewhere at the palace. But was getting stranded in France worth the risk?

"We've come all this way and we're so close to finding the logbook. I know it," said Sofia.

"If you know it, then I know it, too," Sam said, tightening his camera strap. "To the palace we go!"

Sofia tapped the glowing green button with her finger and the touch screen shimmered. Flashes of rainbow light flickered around them like fireworks on a summer night. The electric charge gave Sofia goose bumps.

Sam counted down, "Three . . . two . . . one . . ."

Sofia closed her eyes against the blinding light. Her heart leaped into her throat as the engine grumbled for a split second, and then—

Whiz . . .

Zoom . . .

FOOP!

9
The Cherub's Foot

Sofia opened her eyes and took a deep breath. Although she and Sam had just zipped around the world on the scooter earlier that day, the sensation still made her feel dizzy. She rubbed her eyes and looked around.

A series of majestic buildings lay before them.

"The Palace of Versailles," Sam said.

Sofia looked at the scooter's touch screen. The battery power had dipped to seven percent. "We're really pushing it," she said, a concerned look on her face. "We probably have less than an hour before the battery completely dies."

They hopped off the scooter and walked into a massive courtyard. Hundreds of people wandered the cobblestone, gazing in awe at the magnificent buildings and spectacular plants. The Palace of Versailles was elegant and overwhelming. So much so that Sofia had no idea where to begin looking for the logbook.

"Let's use the map Émilie gave us and follow Monique's directions," Sofia said.

"How are we supposed to do that?" Sam asked.

Sofia took out Philippe's compass. "With this. Maybe the same compass that helped my great-great-great-great-grandfather sail around the world will help us find his logbook."

"'Walk west to the oranges, north-west to the mirror,'" Sam said, reading Monique's note. He took out the map. "We're at the *Cour d'Honneur*, where we're supposed to start."

Sofia held out the compass and slowly turned until she was facing west. They headed in that direction and walked into the exquisite gardens. A tangy scent filled Sofia's nostrils.

"I smell oranges," Sofia said.

"Me too," Sam said. "According the map, this area is the Orangerie."

"We've walked west to the oranges!" Sofia said.

"Let's see if we can find this mirror thing," Sam said.

They followed the compass north-west down a beautiful tree-lined grove. Several tourists wandered among the statues and benches. Off to their right, a small fountain sprayed water into the air. Soon, they came to another body of water with even more fountains.

"Where are we?" Sofia asked.

"The map says this is called..." Sam looked over the pamphlet. "The Mirror Pool!"

"Okay, now we've walked north-west to the mirror," Sofia said.

Confidence bubbled inside her as she looked to her notebook and read the next line. "'Stroll north and the giant sun god will appear here.'"

They used the compass to walk north and, moments later, came upon an even larger fountain. This one had a massive bronze sculpture of a man rising out of the water on a chariot of horses.

"This is Apollo's Fountain," Sam said, looking

at the map. "And Apollo's the sun god in Greek mythology!"

"Three directions down, one to go!" Sofia said.

"What's the next clue?" Sam asked.

"'The Spring Fountain follows, to the opposite of west. Look close for the cherub marked with our dear crest.'"

Sofia looked at the compass. "The opposite of west is east!" she said, and that's the direction they walked.

"Do you see the Spring Fountain?" Sofia asked.

"No," Sam said, shaking his head. "There's nothing on the map named the Spring Fountain."

Sofia felt like she had swallowed a rock. She knew they didn't have much time before the scooter's battery ran out of power. They were about to give up when another fountain came into view. It had a gilded statue of a woman lying on the ground wearing a crown of flowers. She gazed longingly into the sky with four winged cherubs surrounding her.

"What's the name of this fountain?" Sofia asked.

"The map says it's called Flora Fountain," Sam answered. "Not the one we're looking for. And we need to get back to Compass Court."

"Flora . . . flora . . . *flower*," Sofia muttered. "Flowers bloom in the spring. Maybe this is Monique's Spring Fountain?"

Sofia didn't wait for Sam's response. She kicked off her shoes and socks

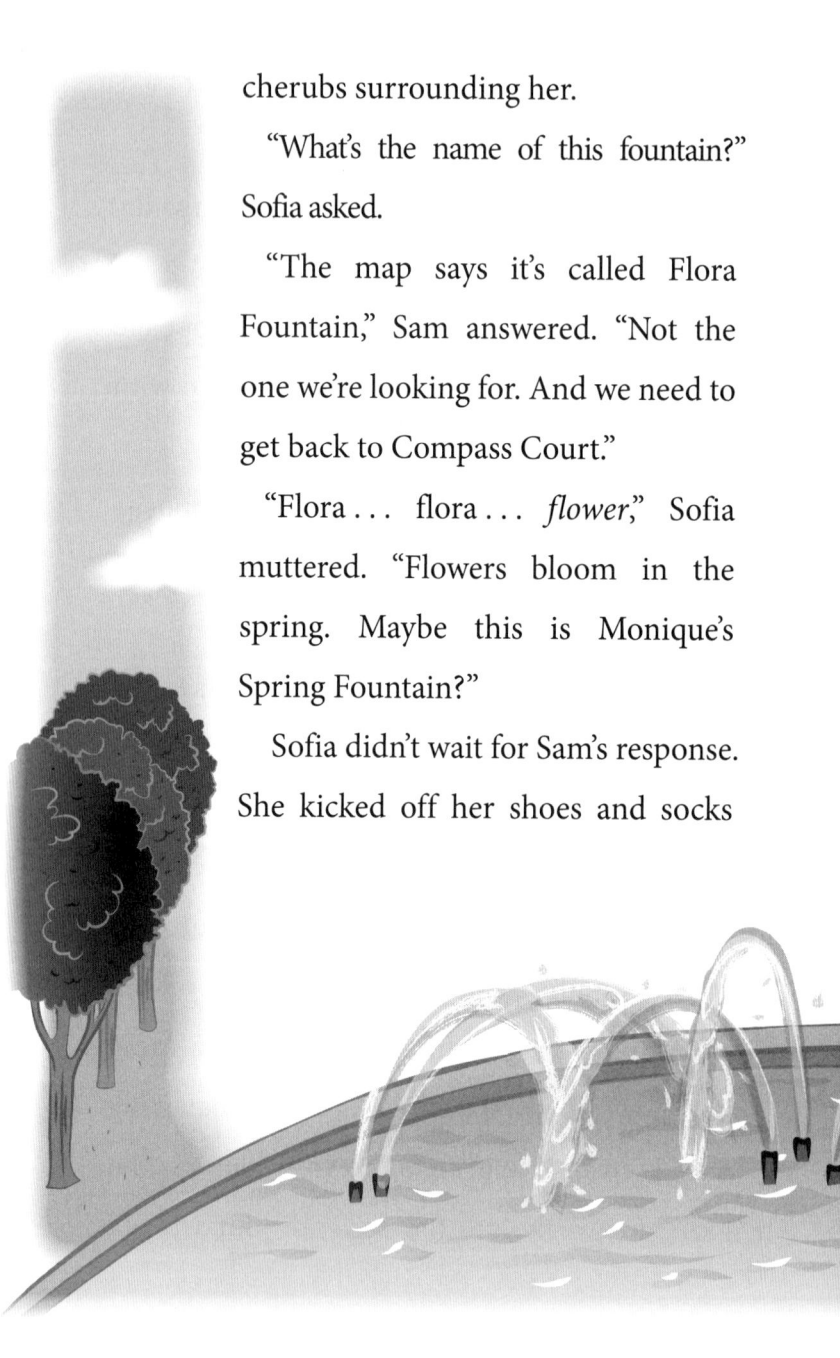

and waded into the waist-high water.

"Get back here!" Sam said.

Sofia trudged through the water and climbed onto the sculpture's platform. She carefully examined each cherub from wing to foot, looking for the family crest.

"Do you see anything?" Sam asked.

"Nothing on the first three," Sofia said. "But there's still one more."

The last cherub was lying on its right side, reaching its arms into the air. Sofia felt along the cherub's body,

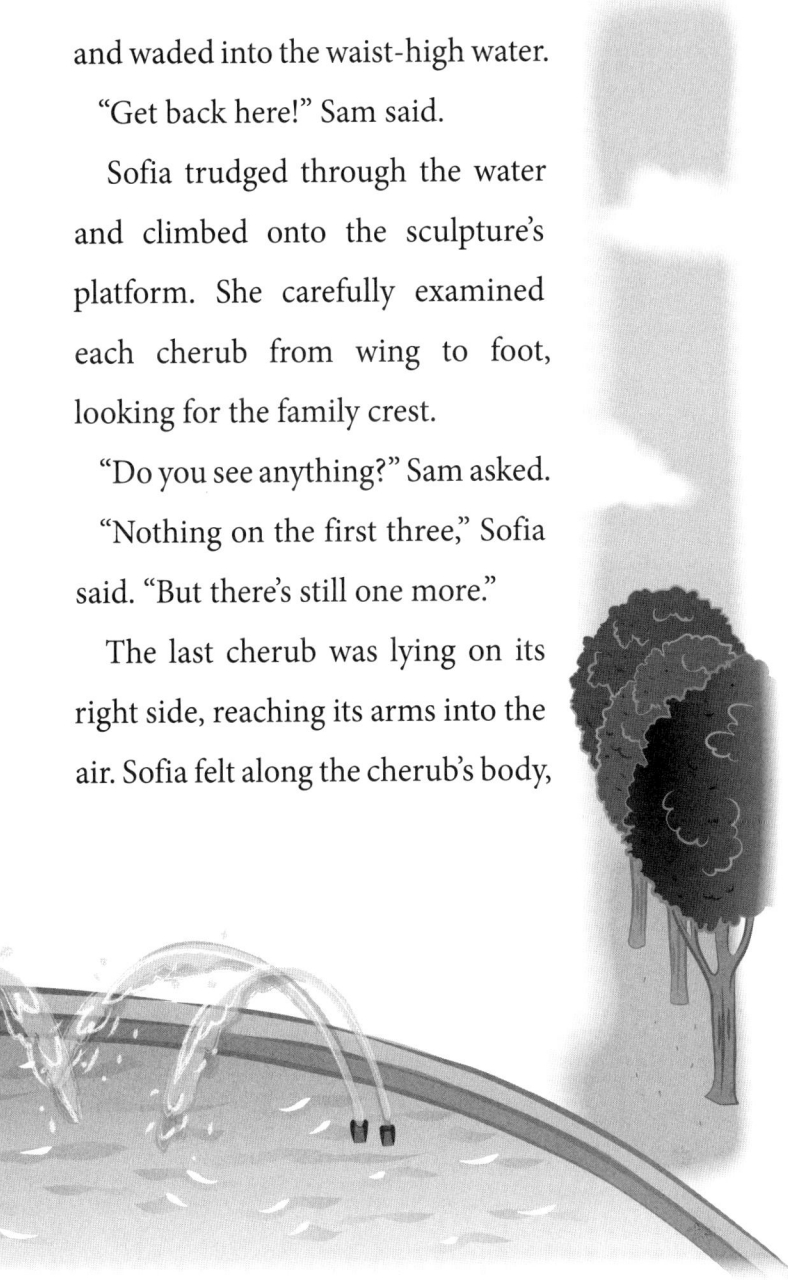

searching for any marks or engravings. Finally, on the cherub's right heel, she felt something with her fingers. Using her shirt, she scrubbed away a layer of dirt and scum until an anchor and two seagulls appeared in the light.

"It's here!" she called to Sam. "I see my family crest!"

The mark on the cherub looked exactly like the back of Philippe's compass. She was just about to yell for Sam to wade out and take a picture when a tiny crack in the bottom of the cherub's foot caught her attention. But the line in the stone looked too neat to be a crack. Sofia gasped. It was a secret compartment! With a gentle tug, she pulled the piece of statue away and revealed a narrow opening.

10
Scooter Shutdown

Sofia reached her hand into the opening and saw a small, very old book bound in leather. She carefully pulled it out, opened the cover, and read the title page.

"Philippe's logbook!" Sofia exclaimed. "We

found it!"

Sofia waded back through the water, holding the book over her head. Her clothes were soaking wet, but she didn't care. They had found Philippe's long-lost logbook, and she couldn't wait to start reading.

She showed Sam the title page.

"It's . . . it's . . ." Sam stuttered, eyes wide with disbelief.

"It was in a secret compartment in the cherub's foot!" Sofia said. "Monique must've hidden it there."

"Hundreds of years ago!" Sam said.

"What an amazing adventure," Sofia said.

Sofia flipped to the table of contents.

"It's written in French," Sam said. "How are we supposed to read it?"

"*Attaque de pirates* sounds like Attack by

Pirates," Sofia said. "And *Brésil* means Brazil ... and *La Mouette* means *The Seagull*. All of the stories are true, Sam! These pages are full! Look at all the adventures Philippe went on!"

"The scooter's touch screen can translate the stories for us," Sam said.

The friends looked at each other at the mention of the scooter.

"The battery!" Sofia said.

They took off down the path, arms furiously pumping, sprinting past fountains, hedges, and flowerbeds. Ten minutes later, they burst out of the *Cour d'Honneur* and into the parking lot.

"Please, please, start," Sofia said, hopping on the scooter.

The touch screen lit up, flashing a red warning sign.

"Hurry!" Sam hollered, climbing behind Sofia. "Hit the button!"

Sofia was so nervous her fingers were shaking. Just before the countdown went to zero, she

jammed her thumb down on the glowing green button. The scooter's powerful engine sputtered for a moment and then rumbled to life beneath them. Its headlights and taillights lit up. The touch screen shined like a shooting star in a midnight sky. A shimmering orb slowly encircled them.

"Farewell, France!" Sofia said.

Whiz . . . Zoom . . . FOOP!

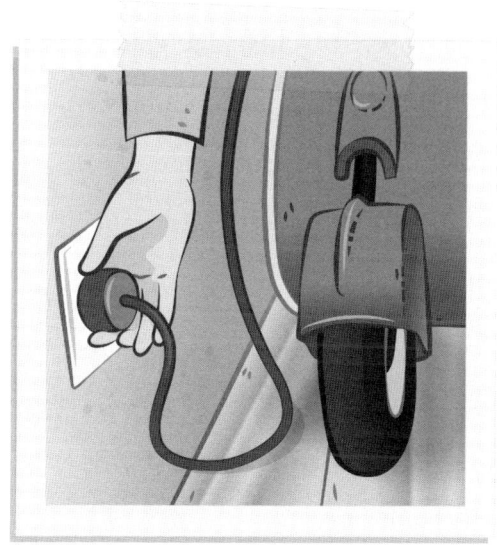

11
Recharging

Sofia and Sam arrived back in Aunt Charlie's workshop with a bone-shuddering **THUD!** Sofia rubbed her eyes and breathed out a big sigh of relief.

"You okay?" she asked Sam.

"Yeah," Sam said, climbing off the scooter. "That was close. Too close. I'm glad we didn't get stuck in France with a dead battery."

"You and me both," Sofia said.

She hopped off the scooter as Sam grabbed a nearby power cord, attached it to the scooter, and plugged it into the wall. Their latest adventure replayed in her mind. They had begun the day looking for things to sell at a yard sale and ended up at the Palace of Versailles. Sofia pulled Philippe's compass out of her pocket. It had stayed hidden in the attic, long forgotten, and now she'd treasure it for the rest of her life.

It seemed fitting that a compass had sparked

such a journey. After all, they lived on Compass Court.

The workshop door opened and Aunt Charlie walked inside.

"Hey, kids," Aunt Charlie said. She looked at Sofia and stopped in her tracks. "You're soaking wet! What have you two been up to?"

Sofia shot Sam a knowing grin.

"Oh, you know," Sofia said. "Just swimming with mermaids and fighting pirates."

"We set sail on the open ocean and visited new lands," Sam said.

"We traveled the world!"

"That sounds like quite a wonderful adventure," Aunt Charlie said. "*Tout est bien qui finit bien.*"

"What does that mean?" Sam asked.

"'All's well that ends well,'" Aunt Charlie said. She smiled. "It's French."

Sofia gave Sam a look as Aunt Charlie sat down at her workbench. "Thanks for plugging the scooter in," Aunt Charlie said. "It probably needs a good charge."

A huge smile spread across Sam's face.

"And something tells me," Aunt Charlie continued, "you two could use some recharging yourselves."

"I feel more energized than ever," Sofia said, clutching Philippe's logbook. "Come on, Sam. Let's do some reading. We have some more exploring to do."

"Feel free to use my photocopier," Aunt Charlie called after them, "in case you need to copy anything."

Sofia remembered Jean-Luc and the promise she'd made to send him a copy of Philippe's sketch. She couldn't help but let out a giggle as Aunt Charlie gave them a wink and returned to her work.

"Thanks, Aunt Charlie," Sam said.

"*Merci*," said Sofia.

And the pair opened the door and stepped out into Compass Court, leaving the scooter in its corner with its touch screen gently glowing.

Fin
(The End)

French Terms

- **Artiste** - Artist

- **Cour d'Honneur** - Court of Honor

- **Couverture** - Blanket or tarp

- **Fermé** - Closed

- **La Mouette** - The Seagull

- **Musée National de la Marine** - National Maritime Museum

- **Non** - No

- **Objet d'art** - Piece of art

- **Orangerie** - Orangery (greenhouse for growing orange trees)

- **Père** - Father

- **Rénovations** - Renovations

- **Restauration** - Restoration

French Phrases

- Ce n'est pas permis. - This is not allowed.

- Étude pour le portrait du Capitaine de Fluerieu - Study for the portrait of Captain de Fluerieu

- Excusez-moi - Excuse me

- Merci - Thank you

- Réservé aux employés - Reserved for employees

- S'il vous plaît. - Please

- Tout est bien qui finit bien - All's well that ends well

Sofia and Sam's Snippets

There are more than 30 bridges throughout Paris. The Pont Neuf was built in 1607 and is the oldest standing bridge crossing the Seine.

FRANCE

Archeologists have discovered stone tools along the banks of the Seine. Some of these artifacts date back thousands of years.

The Seine River is 483 miles long and has been an important commercial waterway since Roman times.

The Eiffel Tower was originally constructed to act as the entrance for the World's Fair in 1889. It weighs over 10,000 tons and is visited by nearly seven million people a year, making it one of the most visited monuments in the world.

The Eiffel Tower

The Statue of Liberty

The Eiffel Tower was designed by and named after engineer Gustave Eiffel. Eiffel also built the frame for the Statue of Liberty in the United States.

The Louvre is the largest museum in the world, housing hundreds of thousands of art pieces. If a visitor looked at each piece of art for only 30 seconds, it would take them 100 days to see everything the Louvre has to offer.

One of the most famous rooms in the Palace of Versailles is the Hall of Mirrors, named after the 357 mirrors found inside. It was here that Germany and the Allied Powers signed the Treaty of Versailles, officially ending World War I in 1919.

The Gardens of Versailles stretch across 2,000 acres, making the area one of the biggest gardens in the world. Millions of people visit the gardens every year.

A variety of plant species grow in the Gardens of Versailles, including orange, lemon, and pomegranate trees from Italy, Portugal, and Spain. Some of the trees are more than 200 years old!

Sections of Philippe's Logbook

- [ ] **I:** Au Départ de France -
  From France

- [ ] **II:** À Travers le Grand Océan -
  Across the Big Ocean

- [ ] **III:** La Tempête endommage la Mouette -
  Storm Damages the Seagull

- [ ] **IV:** Attaque de pirates -
  Pirate Attack

- [ ] **V:** De la voile au radeau -
  From Sailing to Raft

- [ ] **VI:** Débarquement au Brésil -
  Landing in Brazil

Make Your Own Compass

Materials:

- [ ] Small magnet
- [ ] Small paper clip
- [ ] Leaf
- [ ] Shallow dish

Details:

Total Time: 1 hour 10 minutes

Instructions:

1. Fill your shallow dish with water, almost to the brim.

2. Rub one end of the magnet in a single direction along the length of one side of the paper clip. Repeat this step 5-10 times. This will charge your paper clip.

3. Place the charged paper clip on the leaf and carefully float them on the surface of the water.

4. When the leaf stabilizes, the ends of the paper clip will point north and south!

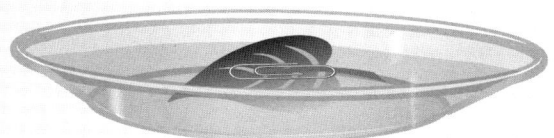